YOUNG WRITERS ANTHOLOGY 2023

Young Writers Anthology 2023

Edited by
LEAH PUGH

ISBN: 978-1-958414-28-6

Twin Sisters Press

Goshen, Kentucky 40026

twinsisterspress.com

OKAMBRIA:

THE FORBIDDEN WORLD

By Annabelle Scott

Dedicated to my dear friend, Cody Toler, who always encouraged the magic inside me.

Okambria was a land that the world had not known for a long time. Every being that walked those once powerful grounds possessed something the world had been afraid of for centuries: magic. Some were blessed with earth magic and could grow the rarest flowers at the blink of an eye or get the fruit trees to bloom even in the dead of winter. Others had fire; they could control the hot bursts of flame and were immune to the heat. There were also those that possessed the magic of the sky.

1

You could always tell who controlled the winds because they sprouted wings. Last, but certainly not least, were those with ocean blue eyes who could bend the waters to their will. Alongside the coveted elemental magic, even the common people possessed the powers of healing, psychic ability, and leadership. Only one magic outweighed it all: the gift of sight. Seers were rarest; there had only been one in the 2,000 years Okambria had been in existence. These extraordinary individuals were given visions of the future... and one can only imagine the benefit and cost of such knowledge.

For centuries, Okambrians lived in peace. Magic was enjoyed and used to help the land flourish. There were lavish fields of every flower imaginable. Rain came every three days to water the crops and flowers. Everyone had a role to play, those roles were fulfilled perfectly.

As time went on, however, the people became irritated with perfect harmony. They wanted change. They wanted a new pattern of living... something unpredictable and adventurous, maybe even dangerous. A group of rebels formed, one of which was a Seer, and they used their magic to wreck chaos. The once peaceful land of Okambria then fell into civil war. It was something none of the people had seen before. They didn't know how to fight; all they had ever known was peace.

A group organized and rose to fight the rebels, but not necessarily with better intentions. This group, naming themselves the Saviors, did take down the rebels with a bloody, hard-fought war... but then banished magic from all of Okambria. They felt magic was the root of the conflict, and anyone who dared to use their powers was executed publicly. The once perfect world quickly fell into ruin. The rain was on no direct schedule, the fields and crops withered and died, and the people were stripped of their freedom.

Okambria's history had been forbidden to be told and thus forgotten. The world, broken for good reason according to the Saviors, was now known as Brokambria. This new land was "safe," yet dreary. The sun rarely shone, and if it did, it was only for an hour or two. The people were forced to work in factories, filling the once blue sky with gray smoke. Instead of fresh crops and hunted meat, they ate bioengineered slop called Kinndup provided by the Saviors. Kinndup was tasteless and gritty in texture. It was despised by all residents, but they knew nothing different. Everyone lived in family groups in what were known as compartments. No matter the size of the family, these small, rectangular buildings had one bedroom, one bathroom, a very small kitchen and living area, and only the necessary furniture, plumbing, and electricity. The Saviors said more was selfish and too individualistic. To maintain perfect harmony, everyone had to be the same.

After several centuries, however, the people grew restless under the unforgiving rule of the Saviors. They yearned for something they didn't know was missing... their innate *magic.* It was like bits of diamond, silver, and gold sewn into their human DNA... but how could one discover it when it was buried so deep within? The Saviors made one grave error in their absolute rule; they assumed no one was ever going to look for magic again.

CHAPTER

ONE

One day a baby girl was born into the land of Brokambria. Her parents, Diana and Finley, named her Valerie, which meant strength. Valerie was strong-willed and brave, even from her youngest years. At barely nine years old, she spoke back to a Savior guard and received the harsh punishment of whipping. She hadn't been allowed back into the factory for months after the offense. When she was allowed to return to work, she was forced to give the guard a public apology. The young girl's face burned with embarrassment, and underneath that, anger and revenge. She silently vowed that she would keep her mouth shut towards the guards until she was older and strong enough to fortify them with action.

By near adulthood, Valerie was the eldest of six sisters.

Katherine, with a shy, calm demeanor came next. Then there was Lisa, a tough little girl who probably would've gotten herself killed before she was five if it wasn't for Diana keeping a close eye on her. Alvara was the next addition; she had green eyes and freckles dancing across her nose and cheeks. She wasn't afraid of the hard work the Saviors demanded, and she had learned exactly what not to do by watching Lisa. Lauren was born a year after Alvara and, taking after Katherine, was extremely shy and compliant. Jaelynn, known better as Jae, was the youngest of the sisters. She, like Lisa, tended to be a loose cannon when unsupervised.

The sisters' lives were far from perfect, but they were good enough for what they knew life to be. Their parents tried their best to provide for them, and their compartment was mostly full of happy memories. It was the little things that mattered, Diana would tell her daughters every time they'd get irritated with their life and wish for new opportunities. Little things like a smile, hug, or rare laugh was all they could cling to after all.

Valerie had only one memory of her mother getting anxious. She had looked in the small, broken mirror in their compartment, and was shocked when her eyes were glowing purple. Valerie ran to show her mom, and her mom quickly grabbed her shoulders and marched her right back to the small bathroom.

"Your eyes aren't glowing, honey, look again," Diana told

her young daughter, her voice shaking. Valerie looked again in the mirror, but the purple was nowhere to be seen. Valerie sighed and walked out, the hope of something new and exciting crushed.

When Jae was twelve years of age, their lives were forever changed for the worse. Their loving parents were executed for overfilling the machine that dished out the Kinndup. Forced to be present, Katherine turned her head away when the executioner, donned in the hideous ceremonial black robe and mask, lifted the axe above his head. She gently shielded the eyes of her younger siblings as well. Valerie, however, stood frozen in the front of the crowd, tears streaming down her cheeks like rain off roofs.

Her blue eyes sought her mother's for the last time, and as the axe came down, the crowd stood silently in respect to their neighbors and in fear of the Saviors. A spark of something never felt before ignited deep inside Valerie. Purple magic, like bursts of lightning, lit up her eyes and radiated out from her whole body. Valerie had heard about this thing called magic, powers that could get you killed if discovered, and she held her breath while glancing at her sisters. Her heart rate sped up when she saw different colors emitting from their bodies as well. Bright shades she had never seen before swelled to fill the gray sky. Trembling in shock and fear, Valerie reached for her sisters, and all of them joined hands. She knew they would be publicly executed because of these bursts of magic; she was sure of it. The crowd closing in around them, only made magical colors coil faster and wider around them. As it reached a dizzying velocity, the sisters gripped each other tighter and tighter... they could hear the crowd screaming. Then in the next moment, everything went black, and they could hear nothing at all.

CHAPTER
TWO

Valerie awoke in a place she had never seen before. She wondered if this was perhaps the afterlife a few of the elders whispered about from time to time. As she took in the stone, windowless walls and cool air, however, she quickly realized she wasn't dead. She was *underground.*

As she gathered her faculties, a rough looking girl she later learned was named Freya started talking a mile a minute. Freya was part of a group who called themselves the Vortex, an underground establishment fixated on taking down the Saviors, freeing the people, and returning Brokambria to its former glory. It seemed that after the sisters' magic burst, Freya and her underground team had used their own magic to rescue them from the Saviors.

Valerie felt the magic burning deep inside her again and

glanced down to see the same purple smoke swirling around her wrists. She noticed a mirror on the wall and looked to see her eyes emitting purple light. It was as though the magic was confirming she finally was in the right place with the right people. She could feel her life's purpose.

It only took the eldest daughter of Diana and Finley seconds to decide that she was going to be a part of this movement. *This* was who she was meant to be, and so began the training. She and her sisters learned that Katherine, glowing with green magic was gifted with psychic abilities; she could read every mind in a room at any given time, but it took a lot of focus at first. Lisa's yellow magic swirled around her body, and wings grew from between her shoulder blades. She touched the pure white feathers, a smile growing on her face as she realized that she had always been special. Fire flickered from Alvara's swirling red fingertips, slowly growing into a large flame as she became more confident in her abilities. Lauren was thrilled when she learned she could heal a small cut with her milky white magic. Larger wounds took more time, but with concentration she became extremely skilled as a healer. With her own swirling blue magic, Jae particularly enjoyed filling glasses full of ice cold water with no water source nearby. The water just poured from her fingertips, and she even managed to freeze it in midair.

Valerie was very different, though. She was a Seer, the first in centuries, Freya confided excitedly. Her first vision was of holding a jeweled sword while standing at the edge of a vast field of vibrant flowers and luscious crops.

"What does it all mean?" Valerie asked Freya when training was completed. Freya, who had grown to be more than a mentor, and was now a dear friend, couldn't contain her hopeful smile.

"What does it all mean?" she repeated before answering the question. "It means that you and your sisters are going to be Okambria's true saviors."

CHAPTER

THREE

Another thing their parents had always taught them was never to fight. It was wrong and dangerous, especially if the Saviors thought there may be a breech to their perfect peace. Emotions were never to be expressed, and if they weren't held back, a public whipping awaited them. Freya had a hard time getting the sisters to realize that in Vortex, emotions weren't only safe to express, but encouraged! With all the new personalities the sisters gave to the small community, it made the Vortex community a much brighter place.

Valerie and her sisters had gone through an intense training program and were now warriors intent on saving a world they never knew personally but wanted to experience with every fiber of their being. They learned how to wield weapons from small knives and swords to guns. Lisa became quite skilled with a bow and arrow, quickly becoming the best archer in Vortex... on land and in the sky. Jae and Alvara were most accomplished at hand-to-hand combat, Alvara unbeatable as she could just burn her opponent. Lauren, who could hit the bullseye every time she threw a knife, preferred to stay on the sidelines and heal any injures. Katherine wasn't particularly skilled in any of these areas, but she could shoot a pistol incredibly well. Valerie, like the version of herself in her vision, was a natural at wielding a sword.

Freya kept a close eye on all six sisters. Once they each became the best in their realm of expertise, she started formulating a plan to defeat the Saviors and return Okambria to its former glory. She didn't exactly know what Okambria had been in the beginning; all she had was stories secretly passed down from the elders. However, she knew that anything they achieved would be better than bitter, oppressed Brokambria.

The plan was formed over a year's time. It consisted of infiltrating the Savior compound, then attacking on their own territory by complete surprise. Without that important element, the attack was bound to be fruitless. They had thought out every possible outcome, gaining approval from even the most reluctant Vortex members, and it was time to put it into action. The first step was for the six sisters, wearing their standard Savior-issued clothes and equipped with their best weapons, to infiltrate the Saviors.

Katrina, one of Vortex's brightest minds, was able to

blend in with the nameless community of Brokambria, and had started working her way up the Savior ladder of leadership six months prior. She was also the one who had cleared the back tunnel, once an old sewage pipe, for the sisters to use to get inside the Savior compound unspotted. She and several other undercover agents would be waiting for them when they got top side, knowing the fight would be worth the cost.

The sisters climbed inside the tunnel, which was damp and had a musty smell, making the sisters scrunch their noses in disgust. As they crawled towards their old home, their magic burned freely inside them. Their time with the Vortex fraction not only taught them how to wield their magic and fight for what was right, no matter how forgotten, but it had changed every single one of them. They now not only yearned for a better life for themselves and all those controlled by the Saviors, but they dared to hope for it. They believed it was attainable.

Valerie paused at the grate leading to the presidential office of the head Savior and looked back at her sisters, hunched in a single file line behind her. A strike of fear raced down her spine. What if not all of them made it out of this battle? Lisa gave her a firm nod. It was a risk they were willing to take. Emboldened by their inborn magic, they were on the cusp of a brand new era... and they knew it.

"Sisters," she whispered quietly. "This is for Mom and Dad. Today we fight, and tomorrow we taste freedom!"

Then she opened the grate.

CHAPTER

FOUR

L ike a fire when it first licks oxygen, Valerie and her sisters were invincible in their fighting that day. As the breach was known and the battle swelled, they only grew higher, dominating their rivals. Saviors rushed in from every direction, but even their strongest army was no match for the sisters' magic, combat skills, and immense heart.

The metal of their weapons clanked against those of the Saviors. Some of the weapons grazed the sisters, but Lauren was ready on the sidelines to fix any wound. Katherine also stayed by the sides, protecting Lauren as she quickly healed any wounds. Alvara was a bit hesitant at first, worried that her fiery magic may get out of control and she would hurt her sisters alongside the enemy. Once a Savior grabbed her wrist, thinking he could disarm her, fire ran down her arm and lit him ablaze, Alvara didn't hold anything back. Valerie swung her sword, the blade cutting through the air and then straight through the Savior she was fighting. Lisa, the only one who could fight from the skies, floated above the Saviors and shot arrows left and right. Jae lured the Saviors into a closed off room, a grin on her face, then locked them inside and flooded the room. With all the different tactics and talent at play, the Saviors didn't stand a chance.

The unexpected fight that broke out in the Savior compound that day went down in history as the Freedom Battle. The sisters had fought valiantly to restore Okambria, and although it could have cost them their lives, it was well worth it in the end. As the sun rose the next morning, Valerie stood atop the ruins of the Savior compound, looking over the new, free land.

Her sisters, each one with minor bruises and cuts, gathered around her, hands on one another's shoulders. A crowd slowly amassed at the scene, surprised and confused. They didn't realize they were looking up at the real saviors of Okambria because they had never known they were captives. Members of Vortex now openly made their way through the crowd, explaining what had happened with smiles and tears of joy. They had waited for this day for so long. A cheer finally started by one small boy, and it grew into a roar. A smile spread across Valerie's face. The same magic that had given her the courage to make a change burned inside her and spun around her wrists.

Valerie glanced down at the battered, slightly bent sword

in her hands, and her purple magic extended out the blade, making it new. When the magic dissipated, the weapon was the one from her vision. The hilt was a bright gold, covered in precious, sparkling jewels, and the blade glinted in the brightening sun. Valerie could see her proud reflection smiling back at her, and she suddenly knew what to say.

She looked over the crowd, the people that had once lived in fear now shouting praises for their new leaders. Valerie knew she had a big job to do. Her eyes found Freya in the crowd, and she knew she wouldn't have to do it alone, though. Another brave burst of magic spurred her forward, and she opened her mouth to shout over the crowd, "Okambrians of the free Okambria! Today is the first day of the rest of our lives. A life of liberty, a life where we are not afraid to embrace the magic we are gifted with. Today, we are one. One people, one land, *one voice!*"

As the crowd raised their hands and cheered ever louder, bursts of colors began to swirl around them and shoot upward like fireworks. Freedom, Valerie decided, was the most beautiful thing she had ever seen.

The End...

Or is it the beginning?

Annabelle Louise Scott, an accomplished young author from Kentucky, has won first place in several local writing competitions in addition to her stories often holding the number one place on Wattpad. Her interest in writing peaked during the COVID-19 pandemic lockdowns of 2020, helping her overcome her own mental health battle. Since then, what started out as a stress-relieving hobby turned into a passionate mode of self-expression – one of her most beloved pieces being "Speak Up; It Could Save Your Life," a suicide awareness article published in a national magazine for homeschoolers.

When not writing, Annabelle enjoys reading dystopian and fantasy novellas, advocating for mental health, spending time with friends, and training her horse, Myra. She especially loves to go on trail rides and jumping courses, and she doesn't even mind mucking stalls!

Annabelle's dream has always been to go to medical school and become an obstetrician. She also hopes to have a family of her own one day. Wherever God leads her, however, she knows writing will remain an important part of who she is.

AULUS

THE SPEAKING TREE

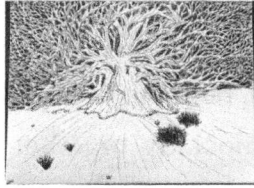

By Maddox Ryan

I was sitting on the ground, leaning against a tree, whistling and whittling a stick as I listened to a burbling stream mosey its way south when the tree that was supporting my back moved!

Alarmed, I dropped my stick and blade and jumped to my feet. The trunk of the ancient tree shook violently, and shed a great amount of leaves in the process. The tree repeated this curious spectacle, and by now, my bare feet, along with all of the grass surrounding the tree, was thoroughly covered in green leaves!

Lifting up each of my feet individually, I shook off the leaves on them, then admired the comfort of this leafy carpet I stood upon. I brushed off the leaves atop my straggly head full of hair, then returned to staring at the quaking tree that stood before me.

After a pause, if my eyes don't deceive me, two bulging hazel eyes appeared a few feet higher than I was in length! The two strikingly large eyes blinked twice, then looked about wonderingly. To my amazement, a handful of inches below the large hazel eyes, a mouth opened, and there came a rumbling noise from within the trunk of the tree. The trunk of the tree gave a loud, belching, burp, then licked its lips.

With my knees knocking together in fear, I stumbled a few paces backward toward the stream. I suddenly slipped on a mossy rock and went tumbling onto my bottom in the shallow, burbling brook. The tree, who had been watching me, looked at me with such perplexed, interested eyes that I doubted the tree had any ill intentions in store for me.

Picking myself up out of the cool water of the stream, I said loudly, "Who are you, and what are you called?"

There was a silence, then the tree said in a rumbling, affectionate voice, "Do you shout so horribly loud all of the time, or is it intended to help me hear you?"

I thought this over a moment, then said loudly, "For you, I suppose, but please, answer my first question!"

The tree shook its branches violently again, then said, "Then do, quiet down! I am in no need of any persons trying to help me hear—my own ears can hear small voices just as well as anyone." Suddenly, there was a loud, cracking noise, and two branch-looking-arms broke free from either side of the trunk of the talking tree.

With my mouth hung open in wonder, I thought of what other mysterious things the days ahead of me held.

"And to answer your first question, I am called Aulus. And if you could answer this question, what are those things protruding from your backside?" Aulus the Speaking Tree listened intently for an answer from me, all the while rubbing one of his lower branches with his branch-looking-arms.

My eyes almost popped out of their sockets. How could any being not know what WINGS were? In fact, I had never come across in my decently lengthy life a being who could speak and didn't have wings! The thought of a being who didn't have wings was simply outrageous!

"They are called wings, my friend! Surely you are pulling my leg?"

Meanwhile, Aulus the Speaking Tree had stopped rubbing one of his branches and stood silent and still. After I had spoken, Aulus the Speaking Tree seemed to enter a sort of daze, which he didn't come out of until I snapped with my thumb and forefinger. He jolted back into reality with a jerk, then cleared his throat.

"I am afraid I don't understand. I clearly haven't touched either of your stubby, little legs."

I frowned at Aulus the Speaking Tree's humorous remark, then looked down at my feet.

"Well, I declare, you haven't touched either of my legs," I murmured to myself.

"What be you called, little winged being?" Aulus the Speaking Tree asked earnestly.

"Wyatt of Bramblebush. And where do you be from?" Said I.

Aulus the Speaking Tree would have been furrowing his brow, if he'd had a brow to furrow. "I guess I am from the forest, I suppose." Aulus the Speaking Tree said after awhile.

"Well, it is becoming darker by the minute. I had better reach Bramblebush before it is too late," said I with a heartfelt sigh.

"No! Wyatt of Bramblebush, please do not leave! I have an errand for you to make." With a crackling sound, Aulus the Speaking Tree bent toward me. "Up in the mountains of Jackle, there is a creature. Its name is Dario the Ogre, and he carries a spiked metal ball on a chain. He is a fearsome animal, with a snout as long as a frying pan that the people of Toothken used in the time of yore."

I could feel the sun leaving the forest as I looked into the eyes of Aulus the Speaking Tree.

"And he is coming to burn this forest, me along with it!"

I felt my knees knocking once again at the burden that was being put upon my shoulders. Stepping back from Aulus the Speaking Tree, I said with as calm a voice I could muster, "Yes, Aulus the Speaking Tree, I will do as you ask."

With tears welling up in my eyes, I dropped to my knees, found my blade that was hidden beneath a layer of summer leaves, then flapped my wings. Rising into the air, I swiveled around and tried to be brave as I flew towards the mountains of Jackle.

～

I AWOKE to the sounds of merry birds chirping and a woodpecker hammering away at some poor old tree. The sun was just peeking over the mountains of Jackle, and I could tell it was going to be a treacherously scorching hot day. Picking myself up out of the bird's nest I had found the nite before, I flapped my wings and rose into the air. Soon, I reached a cave in the side of the mountain, and I flew inside. Landing gently on my feet, I squinted into the darkness. There was a flash of light and a roar.

Treading as lightly as I could, I proceeded toward the flashes of light and the occasional roar of Dario the Ogre. I pulled out my blade from my shirt pocket. Presently, I found myself in a room with shelves filled with bottles, and in the center, there was a pillar with a fire burning on top. Dario the Ogre held his spiked ball on a chain in front of him, and I trembled in fright.

Dario the Ogre roared in anger, finding himself not alone in his home. He stomped toward me, flinging his weapon this way and that.

Finding my task too frightening, I ran back the way I had come. No one brave had ever come out of the small village of Bramblebush, and there never will, I told myself as I fled the horrible monster called Dario the Ogre.

As I flapped my wings in the bright sunlight, I turned. Just as I did so, Dario the Ogre ran off the cliff. In his pursuit of me, he had not heeded the ground below him. Now that there WAS no ground below him, he fell. With a cry of anguish, Dario the Ogre fell . . . fell . . . fell . . . until he hit a rock and landed on a rocky outcropping on the mountains of Jackle.

Flying down to witness Dario the Ogre's fate, I landed on a boulder and looked down on him.

"He was dead all right," I told myself.

With a sigh, I rose into the air. Then, a wonderful thought struck me a heavy blow. In my fright, I had killed Dario the Ogre! I hadn't even had to touch him! Flying gleefully, I smiled as I flew toward the forest where Aulus the Speaking Tree awaited my glorious arrival.

~

I LANDED on the leafy carpet in front of Aulus the speaking tree with a smile on my face.

"Did you destroy Dario the Ogre?" he asked.

"Yes! I did, Aulus the Speaking Tree! I did!" said I joyfully.

It was growing dark, and the cicadas began their song.

"Are you glad I succeeded in killing Dario the Ogre, Aulus the Speaking Tree?" asked I.

"Why wouldn't I be?" asked he in his deep, rumbling voice that I already felt like I knew so well.

"Do you mind if I lean against you?" asked I.

"Of course! You are welcome to," Aulus the Speaking Tree said loudly.

Laughing, I found the stick I had been whittling the day before, leaned against Aulus the Speaking Tree, and began whistling a jolly tune that I thought fit the mood of the day perfectly well, in my opinion.

THE END

Maddox Ryan is from the Kansas City area, though he's been traveling the country with his family for the past couple of years. After living in Arizona, New Mexico, Georgia, Iowa, Wisconsin, and Minnesota. He and his family currently call Kentucky home. He grew up surrounded by and loving books and stories. He started writing at age nine while living on a farm in Kansas, beginning mostly with short stories. He finished his first rough novel at age eleven, doing most of his writing from his bedroom in the attic of an old house in Lawrence, Kansas. He wrote his second novel while living in Georgia, Iowa, Minnesota, Wisconsin, and finished it in Kansas at age fourteen. He wrote Aulus the Speaking Tree the summer of 2021 while living in Des Moines, Iowa. He is an avid reader and especially enjoys reading authors such as

H.G. Wells, D.M. Cornish, N.D. Wilson, and Mark Zusak, along with many others. When he's not reading or writing, you can usually find him drawing, listening to music, or on his skateboard.

HOPE

By Audrey Hackman

S pirit was different from the start. From the moment she was born, she would question every rule on Crescent Island. Her parents would always try to shush her up, but sometimes it didn't work. At those times, her mother had to deal with a lot of visitors from the government, and her father could be found late at night writing words and then crossing them out.

Eventually, Spirit learned to fit in with everybody else, otherwise, it would bring great shame upon the family. She did her work in school quietly and never drew attention to herself, until one day a great scandal arose. On this day, she went to school as usual. The day before, she had submitted a test to become a government official. She was coming to that age where she had to get a job or else the government wouldn't provide food for her anymore. She arrived at school to find that her teacher had posted a list of those who had passed the test. She scanned the list eagerly, becoming more and more desperate as she got closer to the bottom. She read the last name. It was not her. She turned to her teacher.

"Why didn't I pass?" she cried, unable to keep the desperation from leaking into her voice.

"Due to your past behavior, you are not allowed to enter the government," her teacher replied.

All her hopes and dreams seemed to collapse inside her. All she had done was ask questions!

"Who cares about the dumb government?!!" she yelled, and then raced from the room, ignoring the stares and whispers.

She raced home and clambered up the ladder. She burst through her room and buried herself in her pine needle bed. She knew that if you do not get into the government, you must be a laborer. Each government official has a laborer to do their dirty work.

"Spirit!" her mother called, knocking on the door. "You have a message." She slid the message under the door, and Spirit picked it up and read it.

Dear Student Spirit

The government is under the impression that you failed the government test. In that case, from this moment on, you will be a laborer. You will be referred to as Laborer Spirit and will do your work quietly and without complaint. You will be one of the last people to eat and will be the laborer of Councilor Mareeba. Dearest wishes, Councilor Averi.

Spirit tore the letter in half, then tore it in half again until it was demolished. Then she threw the pieces on the floor and stomped on them. Her eyes brimmed with tears. She collapsed on her bed and cried until she couldn't anymore. Then she grabbed the pieces and stuffed them into the trash bin. Her mom knocked on her door.

"It's time to prepare for the Festival of Rebirth," she called.

Spirit had forgotten about the festival. Spirit remembered that it was a festival where the government has a great feast, counts all the people, kills some of them, and makes a speech. While the other people accepted it and didn't think about it, Spirit hated it. She hated watching people get killed. Spirit rinsed off her face and brushed her hair back. She then dipped her finger in the annual red paint made from boiled roses and painted the symbol on her forehead. She slipped on her uncomfortable sandals made from tree bark and stepped out of her door. She made her way down to the meadow where all Festivals are located. There were already lots of people there. Spirit walked to the area where all the Laborers were. It was customary for the Laborers to hand out food to everyone before eating themselves. A Councilor stepped forward.

"We will start this Festival of Rebirth by teaching you all the story of how Crescent Island began. Before Crescent Island was born, there was nothing. Then, the great moon god Luna appeared, shining her light in the dark world. Her brother, the great sun god Elian, was born. They were both children of the great Mother Life and Father Death. Together, they created Earth and ruled together as co-leaders, Elian ruling during the day and Luna during the night. Over time, they had arguments, and then great plagues would terrorize the fish in the seas that covered the earth. However, they grew tired of these fights and soon created people to fight for them. Luna's people lived on Crescent Island, and Elian's people lived on Ray Island. We are now in a time of peace."

With that, the Councilor stepped back, and the Elder Councilor stepped forward.

"Now, the rules. Number one: no eating fruit if you find any. That is saved for the Councilors. Number two: no one is allowed to defy a Councilor. Number three: If you are chosen for execution, do not protest. Number four: eat the food you are given, no matter how moldy the bread is or how dirty the water is. We have no other options." His voice droned on and on until he finally ended at rule 96. "We are now going to announce the executions. There will be five," he announced.

The crowd shuffled uneasily. Five was large for executions.

"Genevieve Damaris. Reason: Random" A wail of shock rose from a young girl who looked about 7.

"Brady Abednego. Reason: Random. Carlos Dagon. Reason: random. Spirit Griffin. Reason: insulting the government."

A wave of shock rolled through Spirit. Ignoring her

parents' horrified stares, she fought her way through the crowd and raced into the woods. She bolted through the woods. She was going to find a boat and ride out into the sea. She got to the harbor and looked at the boats. She chose a small but sturdy one person kayak.

She clambered in and started the familiar stroke with the oars. She remembered when she first learned how to do this when she was 5. Her teacher had told her this was what to do in an emergency. Before long, Crescent Island was out of sight, and the open ocean was all she could see. However, it was late in the day, and she was starting to feel tired after all that had happened. She stopped rowing and lay down in the boat. She drifted off to sleep.

Spirit drearily blinked open her eyes. Her boat was gently rocking, and her confidence was slowly draining. What was she thinking, traveling into the ocean? She glanced at the horizon, and she was filled with dread. Dark clouds were rolling in from the east. She paddled as quickly as she could away from the rain, but she could not move fast enough. She was drenched in minutes. Lightning struck.

Suddenly, a great wave hit the boat, and it was torn to pieces. She clung with all her might to a wood board and could only watch in terror as a great wave bore down on her with the remains of her ship. A wood board struck Spirit on the head, and then everything went dark.

Spirit became aware that someone was shaking her gently. She opened her eyes to find a pair of green eyes looking down at her.

"She's awake!" a voice called, and she was jerked back to reality.

Spirit was on a rocky beach. She was covered with scratches all over, and she was covered in a soft green cloth. She was filled with wonder as she observed the cloth. It was like the softest grass woven together. She looked up at the person who had awoken her and froze. He was covered in the type of cloth. To be that rich, he must have been some type of Councilor. She was only allowed to wear clothes made from pine needles, which were prickly and uncomfortable. She hastily got to her feet and bowed low to the ground. She looked back at him and realized that he was looking at her, confused.

"Would you like some food?" he asked and held up a brightly colored fruit.

Spirit was amazed. This Councilor would offer her fruit? She gratefully accepted it and bit into it. It was paradise. The juice of the fruit seeped into her tongue, and it was surprisingly crispy. It was wonderful. She bit into it again and enjoyed the same experience.

"Are you a Councilor?" she asked him. He looked puzzled.

"What's a Councilor?" he asked.

Spirit was very confused. Who was this man who wore strange pelts, had fruit at his disposal, and who didn't even know what a Counselor was?

"Are you familiar with Crescent Island?" Spirit asked carefully. If this was a person of Elian, then she could very easily insult him.

"No," he replied. "Why, is that where you come from?"

Spirit wanted to learn more about this man's life. The only conclusion she could come to was that her Councilors had lied to her or didn't know, as she could see this man was not lying.

"Show me where you live," Spirit said.

He shrugged and led her to a stone structure on top of the ground instead of in the trees. Spirit followed him inside and stopped immediately. In front of her was the most luxurious house she had ever seen. There was a bed made from that same type of cloth, which made Spirit wonder where he got all that cloth from. There was a surface made from shiny stone, which Spirit was fascinated by, as she didn't have any shiny stone on her island. The floor was made from more of that shiny stone. 5 pieces of fruit were laid out on the surface, which Spirit eyed hungrily.

There was also another shiny surface that ran along the wall. An array of bizarre objects were on this surface. There was a basin in the middle of it with a metal tube above it. There was a box with numbers on the side and a door handle on it. There was also a black shiny thing on the side with numbers on it also and a surface on top with dotted circles on it. Beside the surface, there was a tall rectangular box with two door handles on it, one on the top and one on the bottom. The man stuck out his hand to her.

"I just realized I haven't introduced myself yet. My name is Jacob," said Jacob.

Spirit stared at his hand, unsure what to do with it, then,

on a sudden inspiration, seized his hand in hers and started swinging it back and forth. He stared at her in confusion.

"What are you doing?" he asked Spirit.

She suddenly realized that this wasn't a polite form of greeting. She withdrew her hand and said, "Sorry."

Jacob laughed and said, "It's alright. So where are you from?"

Spirit felt a sudden desire to confide in this man, to tell him about her world. Spirit had never actually talked to anyone, never told anyone what she thought. Spirit told Jacob about her life, how she wasn't allowed to do anything, and that she had almost been killed. He was a very good listener and didn't interrupt at all. When she got to the end, he was looking at her with a very somber look on his face. Then he started to tell Spirit about his world.

When he was finished, she said excitedly, "I'm so excited to try this pasta and meatballs you're telling me about. And the theme parks and zoos..."

"We'll start introducing you to Abranem's wonders tomorrow. Right now, you need to get some rest." Jacob said.

He rummaged under his bed and pulled out a deflated rubber object. He stuck his mouth on it and blew, and before long, it turned into a bed fit for a queen. Spirit tried to lay down in it, and her whole body sank down in it. It was so comfortable that she fell asleep right then and there.

Spirit had lain awake for hours, excited for the day ahead. She now got out of her bed and went to see if Jacob was awake yet. She slipped into his room and saw he was fast asleep. She tried to exit quietly but accidentally knocked over a book on his desk. It crashed to the floor. She returned it to his desk and tried to sneak out, but the damage was done.

He said sleepily, "Spirit? What are you doing up this early?"

She said, "I'm too excited for the day ahead. Can we get going?"

He laughed and responded, "Sure. Just give me a couple of minutes to get ready."

Spirit had already gotten ready, so she waited by the front door, admiring the objects she now knew to be machines.

Jacob stepped over to her and said, "First stop: the theater!"

They stepped out the door and walked toward another machine, which Jacob called the Skydrift. The Skydrift was a device that one stood in and flew. Spirit fidgeted nervously as they secured her feet, and then they were off! Spirit felt the wind rush against her face and laughed aloud. It took them straight to a spacious building. Jacob opened the door, and a blast of cool, refreshing air took Spirit by surprise. She stepped inside and admired the immensity of it.

She barely had time to admire as Jacob swept straight through and came to a stop in front of a door labeled 2A. He opened the door, and she walked inside the warm, dark room. She settled herself in a comfy chair amidst the crowd of people and waited for something to happen. Suddenly,

Spirit heard a noise, but not like someone talking. It was like a bird singing, but many birds singing in harmony.

She listened to the sound and felt her emotions swaying with the tune. She saw people on the stage, moving their body in flowing movements. They moved so gracefully she started to think their bodies were made of air. Then the music stopped, and the crowd erupted, hitting their hands together. She hit her hands together as hard as she could and was surprised by how much it stung. She concluded that she would not hit her hands together, as it hurt a lot, and she didn't know how these people could bear it. However, she thoroughly enjoyed the performance.

She walked out of the theater and boarded the Skydrift, excited for the next part of her adventure. She was getting rather hungry, and she told Jacob, so they stopped at *Stupefi-ante, France.* She was amazed by how good the food was, and when she tried chocolate mousse, she almost fainted.

She exited the restaurant and said, "Jacob, what's next?"

Jacob chuckled merrily and said, "You'll see."

They boarded the Skydrift, and it took them to a park with metal beams everywhere.

"Welcome to your first theme park!" Jacob exclaimed.

Suddenly, on one of the metal beams, a cart came whizzing. Spirit's mouth was in a perfect O. Jacob led her to a line waiting for The Yellowjacket. Spirit read the review as they were waiting.

The sign scared her a lot. Spirit did not think she was going to enjoy it. That sounded terrifying! She was about to tell Jacob she didn't want to go on it when the coaster rolled into the station. It was her turn! She nervously climbed into the seat, shaking all over. She vaguely heard a voice telling her to enjoy the ride, and then they were off! It was going rather slowly, and she thought she might enjoy it.

Then she noticed the huge hill they were climbing up. She came to the very top of the hill, and the roller coaster immersed her in total darkness. Then it dropped! The roller coaster dived and turned and dropped, and she enjoyed it immensely. She got off the coaster with her head spinning.

"So, how did you like it?" asked Jacob.

"That was... so much fun!" Spirit exclaimed. "Can we do it again?"

Jacob laughed.

"Sure, if you want to," Jacob responded.

Spirit rode on roller coasters the rest of the afternoon. By dinnertime she was wiped out.

"Do I get to try pasta and meatballs?" she asked.

"Of course," replied Jacob.

They went into a fancy restaurant and ordered pasta and meatballs. A waitress came with their food. Spirit inhaled the aroma of the meal and couldn't wait to dig in. She snatched a fork and, took a huge serving of pasta and gobbled it down. Her eyes grew wide. Spirit took forkful after forkful of the meal until she was stuffed full, and then some. Her eyes grew even wider when the server brought in a plate filled with a lump of something she had never seen before. It looked like it was melting. She cautiously took a bite and immediately took the bowl and licked the lump vigorously.

Jacob said, "So you're enjoying the ice cream, huh?"

Spirit nodded, licking the bowl clean. She set the bowl down and yawned. "I'm ready to go to sleep," She said.

They quietly rode the Skydrift back to Jacob's house, and she collapsed on the air mattress. As she lay on her mattress and reflected on the day, she couldn't stop thinking about all the hopeless people on Crescent Island. Anger at the Councilors boiled inside her. Spirit promised herself she would go back and bring this happiness to her people. First, though, she had to prove the Councilors were keeping this from them.

Spirit stretched and yawned, squinting at the bright sunlight streaming through the windows. She suddenly remembered what she had planned for that day. She quietly got out of bed and walked into the kitchen. Her plan was to leave quietly so that she would not wake Jacob and go through his protests, but he was in the kitchen already. He was preparing something that smelled delicious.

"I wanted you to try pancakes and bacon before you go," he said.

Spirit gasped. "How did you know?" she asked.

"I knew you couldn't stay while knowing people were suffering. I prepared a bag for your journey," he replied.

He handed Spirit a green backpack. She looked inside and found food, water, and a vest.

Spirit lifted the vest out of the backpack and asked, "What's this for?"

"It's a flotation device, in case you fall in," he responded. "Breakfast is ready!"

She sat down in one of the chairs and watched as Jacob lifted a pan filled with flat, circular cakes onto the table. He also put on the table a pan of long, crispy strips. Spirit had no idea what these were, but she couldn't wait to try them. Jacob had prepared a plate for her, so she started eating. On her plate was a kind of gloopy sauce.

When she asked Jacob about it, he said, "You were supposed to dip your pancakes in it."

Spirit tried it, and it tasted so good. The bacon tasted good, too. She ate quickly and told Jacob she needed to go. He gave her his boat, and she left. Further on in the day, she ate the food and, drank the water, and found a device in the pack with a projector that the device fit into. Attached to the device was a notecard.

'This is a device that records sound and video. I thought you might need it. Jacob.'

Spirit got to the island and found nobody there. She snuck into the woods and found she was on the far side of the island, the Councilors' side. She snuck further and saw all the Councilors in a meeting together. She listened and then turned the device on.

"Have we gotten our shipment of food yet from Abranem?" a hushed voice whispered.

"Yes," someone else responded. "Remember, don't let

anything slip to the people that we're getting good food and luxuries. They need to remember that we're in control. Also, don't eat too much. There can't be rumors of us being overweight."

The others nod and murmur agreement and then disperse. Spirit couldn't believe she caught the whole thing on the device. She snuck into the control area and saw the emergency button, which has everybody come to the meadow. Without any hesitation, she pressed it. Immediately, a loud siren went off everywhere, and cries of panic erupted. Spirit headed to the meadow, where crowds of people were already gathering. She stepped on the stage where only Councilors were allowed, and a hush fell over the crowd. She slid her device into the projector, and the video was projected on the screen.

At the end of the video, the crowd erupted. They started to attack the councilors, punching them, kicking them, pushing them. By the time the crowd had calmed down, the Councilors were beaten bloody. They ran for the boats, and a great cheer arose. Finally, there was hope.

Audrey Hackman is an eleven-year-old crazy cat lady who loves music and reading, particularly fantasy novels. In addition to playing piano and flute, she reads so many books her mom is afraid she is addicted to reading. She wants to be a musician, author, or actress when she grows up. If you see her in her house, she is most likely cuddling with her cat Christopher while reading a book on the couch. She lives in Louisville with her mom, dad, two siblings, cat, dog, and fish. She started writing stories about a year ago and has been homeschooled since COVID. Influenced by The Hunger Games, she wrote this story specifically for the competition.

79942454R00030